Tight Spaces

by Lucy Monroe

Tight Spaces

Lucy Monroe

Lucy Monroe LLC

For the boys –Zach and my own superhero, Tom. You inspire and
bring joy to my life.

Chapter One

D anusia wiggled the key in the lock on her brother's apartment door. Darn thing always stuck, but he wouldn't make her another one. Said she didn't come to stay often enough for it to matter.

Yeah, and he wasn't particularly keen for that to change either, obviously. He'd probably gotten the wonky key on purpose. Just like the rest of her older siblings, Roman Chernichenko kept Danusia at a distance.

She knew why he did it at least, though she was pretty sure the others didn't.

Knowing didn't make her feel any better. Even in her family of brainiacs, she was definitely the odd one out. They loved her, just like she loved them, but they were separated by more than the gap in their ages. She was seven years younger than her next youngest sibling. An unexpected baby, though never unwanted – at least according to her mom.

Still, her sister and brothers might love her, but they didn't get her and didn't particularly want her to get them.

Which was why she was coming to stay in Roman's empty apartment rather than go visit one of the others, or Heaven forbid, her parents. She did not need another round of lectures on her single status by her *baba* and mom.

The lock finally gave and Danusia pressed the door open, dragging her rolling suitcase full of books and papers behind her. The fact the alarm wasn't armed registered at the same time as a cold cylinder pressed to her temple.

"Roman, I swear on Opa's grave that if you don't get that gun away from me, I'm going to drop it in a vat of sulfuric acid and then pour the whole mess all over the new sofa Mom insisted you get the last time she visited. If it's loaded, I'm going to do it anyway."

The gun moved away from her temple and she spun around, ready to lecture her brother into an early grave, and help him along the way. *"It is so not okay to pull a gun on your sister..."* her tirade petered off to a choked breath. *"You!"*

The man standing in front of her was a whole lot sexier than her brother, and scarier, which was saying something. Not that she was afraid of him, but *she* wouldn't want him for an enemy.

The rest of the family believed that Roman was a scientist for the military. She knew better. She was a nosy baby sister after all, but this man? Definitely worked with Roman and carried an aura of barely leashed violence. Maxwell Baker was a true warrior.

She shouldn't, absolutely *should not*, find that arousing, but she so did.

"You're not my brother," she said stupidly.

Which was so not her usual mode, but the six-foot-five black man, who would make Jesse Jackson Jr. look like the ugly step-brother if they were related, turned Danusia's brain to serious mush.

His brows rose in mocking acknowledgment of her obvious words. "Um..."

"What are you doing here, Danusia?" Like a really good, aged whiskey, even his voice made her panties wet.

How embarrassing was that? "You know my name?"

Put another mark on the chalkboard for idiocy.

"The wedding wasn't so long ago, I would not have forgotten already." He almost cracked a smile.

She almost swooned.

Max and several of Roman's *associates* had done the security on her sister, Elle's, wedding, which might have been overkill. Or not. Danusia suspected stuff had been going on that neither she, nor her parents, had known about.

It hadn't helped that she'd been focused on her final project for her Masters, and that Elle's wedding had been planned faster than Danusia could solve a quadratic equation. She'd figured out that something was going on, but that was about it. This time her siblings had managed to keep their baby sister almost completely in the dark.

A place she really hated being.

Not that her irritation had stopped her from noticing the most freaking gorgeous man she'd ever met. Maxwell Baker. A tall, dark, dish of absolute yum.

Once she had seen Max with his strong jaw, defined cheekbones, and big muscular body, not much else at the wedding had even registered. Which might help explain why she hadn't figured out why all the security.

"It's nice to see you again." There, that sounded somewhat adult and full points for polite conversation, right?

"What are you doing here?" he asked again, apparently not caring if he got any points for being polite.

She shrugged, shifting her backpack. "My super is doing some repairs on the apartment."

"What kind of repairs?"

"Man, you're as bad as my brother." They hadn't even made it out of the entry, and she was already getting the third-degree.

Really as bad as her brother and maybe taken up a notch. Roman might have let her get her stuff put out of the way before he started asking the probing questions. Then again, maybe not.

"I'll take that as a compliment." Then Max just waited, like he had all the time in the world to wait for her answer.

Like it never even occurred to him she might refuse to do so.

Knowing there was no use in attempted prevarication, she sighed. "They're replacing the front door."

"Why?"

"Does it matter?" Sheesh.

He leaned back against the wall, crossing his arms, muscles bulging everywhere. "I won't know until you tell me."

"Someone broke it." She was proud of herself for getting the words out considering how difficult she was finding the simple process of breathing right now.

This man? Was lethal.

"Who?" he demanded, frown firmly in place.

Oh, crud, even his not-so-happy face was sexy, yummy, heart palpitatingly delicious. "I don't know."

"A break-in?" he asked in that tone her brother got sometimes, the one she secretly called his *work* voice.

"An attempted one, yes. Whoever it was didn't expect the crazy loud alarm Elle installed the last time she visited."

Neither had she. It had woken Danusia from an exhausted sleep after too many hours going over research data. If her heart wasn't so healthy, it would have stopped.

She only hoped whoever had tried breaking in and disturbed her sleep hadn't been so lucky.

"You don't talk like a professor."

"That's because I'm a student." Sort of. She was an Assistant Professor during the school year, but it was summer, and she was firmly in researching student mode.

"Roman said you're getting your PhD."

She shrugged. Playing down her academic accomplishments was a long-held habit for her.

He looked her up and down. "You're pretty young to be going for your doctorate, aren't you?"

"Not if you consider I started college when most of my peers were starting high school." When even being reminded of how out of step with her peer group she was didn't dampen his effect on her libido, she was in serious trouble.

"That's my point."

"Point?"

"Don't play dumb, professor. We both know you're smarter than that."

"Don't call me professor."

He just gave her a look.

"Being younger than my peers is bad enough, I don't need to talk like a total geek, on top of it." The normal college student speak was something she worked diligently on. It was too easy to let five-syllable words slip into the conversation when she wasn't thinking about it.

"Why not? You should be proud to be so intelligent."

"I am more than my brain." Not that other people seemed to realize that.

Sometimes, even her family, as wonderful as they were, tended to treat her like an extension of her IQ. They were all highly intelligent, but the fact that she'd outdone them all academically put her inside a bubble that could get really lonely.

Not that she ever complained. She wouldn't disappoint her family for the world. And being anything less than grateful for all the opportunities for the amazing education that she'd had would do that.

"Why didn't you just stay in a hotel overnight?" Max asked, apparently dismissing the subject of her smarts.

Thank goodness.

"The super wasn't sure he'd get to the door right away." And she hadn't wanted to stay in the apartment alone right now.

Her roommate wouldn't be back until a few days before fall term started and that was weeks away. Rebekah had gone home for the summer, while Danusia had opted to stay on and work on the research for her doctoral thesis.

The attempted break-in had shaken her; not that she'd admit that to anyone else.

"Bullshit. A new door for you is his top priority."

"Now you really sound like my brother." And she didn't feel sisterly toward Max. Not even a little.

"Do you want me to talk to your super?"

"I'm perfectly capable of handling this on my own," she gritted out. She was not his little sister, and even if she had been, Danusia was twenty-four. "I'm an adult, or hadn't you noticed?"

Something flared in his gaze that sent butterflies on suicide bombing missions in her stomach. "I noticed."

"I don't need anyone talking to my super for me, not you, not my brother. Understood?"

Amusement curved his lips and he saluted, way too precisely for him to be anything but true military. "Understood, ma'am."

She laughed. "Oh, knock it off."

"You've got Roman's temper."

"Most people think my brother doesn't have a temper." He was too cold to be considered temperamental.

"I've known him a long time."

"You haven't known me very long, but you've already sussed out one of my secrets."

He shrugged, those big, muscled shoulders rolling and pulling his dark t-shirt taut across his perfectly defined pecs. "What can I say? I'm good."

"No arguments here." She gave him a look, doing her best to let him know she didn't just mean his interrogation techniques.

His eyes widened and then narrowed. "Save that for your college boy friends."

"I don't have any."

"You don't have any male friends?"

She didn't have very many friends at all, but that wasn't what she meant. "I don't have a boyfriend."

"So, get one."

That had her laughing out loud. "Right, like that's going to happen."

"Shouldn't be too hard. You're wicked smart. You're sexy." He did that shrug-thing again.

She wasn't sure if it was the shrug, or his words, but her heart felt like it had started practicing for the Grand Prix. "You think I'm sexy?"

"Don't let it go to your head. I'm sure a lot of guys do."

"Now, I know you're just being nice. Guys do not think geeky PhD students are sexy."

He reached for the handle on her rolling case. "If you say so. You'll have to sleep in Roman's room. I'm in the guest room."

He started walking down the hall toward the bedrooms, tugging the overloaded case like it was filled with nothing more than air.

"Why are you staying here?"

"I gave up the lease on my apartment, but the condo I bought and was supposed to move into won't be ready for another two weeks."

"The builder is running behind?" she asked, wondering who in their right mind didn't keep their commitments to a man like Maxwell Baker.

"Yeah, but we negotiated a twenty-thousand dollar drop in my condo price because of it. It's all good."

She'd just bet they'd negotiated.

He deposited her suitcase at the end of Roman's king-size bed. She dropped her backpack with her clothes in it on the corner of the mattress closest to her.

He looked at the backpack and then at her suitcase. "Let me guess, clothes in the pack and books in the heavy-as-hell case."

"I told you. Geek."

"Serious student, anyway. How close are you on your thesis?"

"I've still got some research to go through, but I should be ready to present and defend by the end of October."

"That's still a few months out."

"It's a doctoral thesis, not a term paper, or so my advisor keeps saying."

"Sounds like a hardass."

"I'm sure Dr. Shay would appreciate you saying so. I'm convinced she works on her scary factor in front of the mirror at night."

"So, what's this thesis on?"

"The use of nanotechnology in pharmaceuticals." Which was something that fascinated and delighted her, but usually caused glazed eyes and yawns in other people.

"I didn't think we were there yet."

"We're closer than a lot of people realize."

"You and Spazz would have a lot of fun talking this technical shit."

"You mean Lieutenant Kennedy?"

"That's the one."

"He's really...um...hyper."

"On coffee? He's all sorts of scary."

"So, the nickname, Spazz?"

"Yes."

"What do they call you?"

"Luke."

"Luke?" What kind of nickname was that? Then she thought for a second. Unable to believe she hadn't gotten it right away, she asked, "Like in Luke Cage, the superhero, super strong with skin impervious to almost any weapon?"

"Yep."

She looked him up and down, making no effort to hide her perusal, but doubting it had the same effect on him as his in the hall had on her. "I can see it, but why not call you Power Man?"

"You know your superheroes."

She felt a blush climb her cheeks. "I like comic books."

"You've got to more than *like* them to know the details of Luke Cage."

"Born Carl Lucas, came by his powers in a military experiment gone wrong and first appeared in *Luke Cage, Hero for Hire*. One of only a handful of black superheroes in either the Marvel or DC comic universes."

Max was grinning by the time she was done reciting the basic facts of one of her favorite superheroes. "Like I said, sexy, professor. Very sexy."

Not only was his nickname from Power Man, but he thought her closet superhero obsession was sexy? Oh, this man was perfect for her, now she just had to convince him of that fact.

Not that she had a clue how to go about doing that. Her dating record was sketchy at best. She'd had blind date disasters instigated by her family and Rebekah, but that wasn't the same as participating in the mating dance with a man that she had the hots for.

But Danusia had never even kissed a man she was attracted to. Oh, she'd been kissed. She'd even had sex. Disasters didn't get that designation lightly, after all.

But this was different. When she'd met Max at the wedding, Danusia had been sure he was way out of her league. That a geek like her wouldn't even register on his radar. Now he was telling her that she wasn't just a blip, but she was a sexy one.

Oh, wow. Oh, wow. Oh, wow.

Would fainting prompt him to give her the kiss of life and would that start something she'd only be too happy to finish?

"What are you thinking about?" he asked suspiciously. "You've got a strange look in your eye and your brother warned me about you."

That was the second time he'd admitted to talking to her brother about her. That had to mean something, right? That he was at least interested enough to mention her in passing to Roman.

"What did he warn you about?"

"That you have an unbalanced sense of humor."

"Unbalanced? That's harsh." Though Roman had said worse when she'd switched salt for sugar in his canister and he'd added it to his morning coffee.

It was an old trick, and she shouldn't have gotten away with it, which is what she told him. Sugar and salt didn't look alike to a person with their background in chemistry, not to mention the different smell, texture and melting rate in hot water.

He'd told her she needed to get a life. Of course, it was his effort to see she had one that had prompted the salt in his coffee. He'd fixed her up with the most boring, obnoxiously intelligent man she'd ever met the night before. To make matters worse, they'd gone on a double date and while her brother was having fun with his not-so-brainy arm candy, Danusia had spent the evening arguing quantum physical theory. Not discussing, but arguing.

Her blind date had been an opinionated cretin.

"Do I have to worry you're going to sabotage the kitchen?" Max asked, proving Roman *had* been telling tales.

"I don't know. Are you going to try to fix me up with the most obnoxious man on the Eastern Seaboard?"

"Is that what Roman did?"

"Yes. And when you're contemplating murder, salt in the coffee doesn't seem like such a harsh retaliation."

Max laughed out loud. "I can promise you; I've got no plans to fix you up with anyone while you're here."

"Good." She had her own plans and they all revolved around the gorgeous black man whose laugh made her thighs clench.

Weird. Was that a primal reaction, she wondered, or an evolutionary one? Whatever it was, there was an ache between her legs that would not go away.

"You're doing it again."

"What?"

"Thinking about something that puts that alarming expression in your eyes."

"Do I worry you?" she asked in disbelief.

"More than you know." With that, he spun on his heel and headed out of the room, stopping at the doorway. "I'll make dinner tonight."

"You don't trust me to cook?"

"Let's just say I'll be sure what goes into it, if I make it."

"I'll have you know I'm a very good cook." It was basic organic chemistry, and she'd had that particular subject down before she'd been out of training bras.

"When you aren't switching ingredients on the unsuspecting."

"I told you, he deserved it."

"And I don't."

"Not yet," she couldn't resist saying.

He laughed again and she decided that sound could become more addictive than McDonalds French fries.

Chapter Two

Max julienne sliced the carrots while he reminded himself all the reasons why the sexy little doctoral student currently studying in the living room was off limits.

One - despite her advanced education, she was six years younger than him. Two - that education disparity was just another reason that nothing between them could work. After barely graduating high school, he'd gone directly into the Marines and learned how to kill people. No amount of reading and online courses since then could bridge the gap between the two of them.

And hell, why bridge a gap for a casual fling?

Which was the next biggest reason he needed to keep his hands to himself. Three - Max didn't do serious, and Danusia Chernichenko deserved more than a casual roll in the sack, no matter how hot it was. And it would be desert at high noon hot, too.

He wanted to undo the dark brown hair she always wore in either a long ponytail or braid down her back and bury his fingers in the silky strands. Damn if it didn't make him some kind of walking cliché, but he wanted to see that long dark hair spread out under her while he drove into her small, but curvy body over and over again.

While she shared the rest of her family's pale coloring with almost black hair, unlike the rest of them, Danusia wasn't more than average in height. She couldn't be more than five and a half feet tall with bones like a sparrow.

Too fragile for a man like him, but that didn't stop him wanting her.

Hell, if she didn't deserve more than he could ever give though.

The biggest reason, she was off-limits? Four - she was his friend and team leader's baby sister. A smart man did not play with that kind of fire. It was likely to burn him to ashes for his trouble.

And five – if he needed a five, was that they didn't even live in the same state. Not that he spent a lot of time here, but it was home.

Which again implied he was thinking long term, which he wasn't. Because he never did. He'd lived his whole life watching his mom struggle with what amounted to single parenthood while his daddy spent weeks on the road as a long-haul trucker.

Max's job not only took him away for weeks at a time, but there was no guarantee he'd come back. His missions were dangerous, if necessary.

He wasn't putting a woman through that kind of pain, or himself through the struggle between his job and his family. His daddy's weeks on the road had taken their toll on him as well and he'd died young from a heart-attack.

Max wasn't following that path, no way, no how.

But, damn, he wanted Danusia. Had wanted her at Elle's wedding and the hot need had only grown since. He might not have seen Danusia in the intervening time, but he'd dreamt about her. A lot.

Which was just plain crazy.

Even crazier, he'd pictured her face on more than one woman's body as he was screwing them. It didn't make him proud either. He might not do serious, but he respected the women he had sex with and knew it was wrong to bury his cock in one woman's body while thinking of another one.

Which went a long way in explaining why he'd gone without sex for longer than he had since his first time with the divorcee who lived across the hall when he was fifteen.

His agitated thoughts did not stop him from noticing the muted sounds the moment she stood up and started moving around in the other room. He knew she'd come into the kitchen before her sweet, floral scent told him she'd moved into his personal space.

She leaned around him. "Looks good. Can I help with anything?"

"I've got it."

"I really am a decent cook."

"You're a Chernichenko. I doubt there's anything you don't do well."

She laughed, but the sound was more sad than humorous. "Isn't it obvious? I'm not like the others."

Sliding the carrots into the steamer, he fought the urge to turn around. And lost. He put the lid on the cooking vegetables and then turned to face Danusia.

She was mere inches away and it was all he could do not to reach out and pull her the remaining distance so their bodies connected. "What do you mean?"

She rolled her eyes and stepped back. "You don't have to pretend to be nice. I know my limitations."

What the hell? "Don't you know how proud of you Roman is?"

"Sure. I'm the freak among freaks, right? My siblings are so smart, they scare people and I'm even smarter. That's really something great, isn't it?"

"I guess it depends on what you do with that big brain of yours." But he didn't like her sad, almost weary tone.

"My cranium capacity is no larger than average for a woman of my height."

He shook his head. "That's not what I meant."

The amusement now lurking in her grey gaze said she knew that and was teasing him. She didn't dwell on whatever bothered her and while he found that admirable, he didn't like the idea that she carried a burden like that about herself.

"You are something special, Danusia."

"I'm a freak." She shrugged. "But we take the bad with the good, right? If I can be like Matej and develop something to make the world a better, or safer, or healthier place, then it's worth it to be such a bad fit with other people."

"You fit just fine with me."

"And you are a good friend to my brother."

"He's not here now and I still like spending time with you."

"So, give me something to do."

"Tired of studying?"

"You could say that. The latest batch of research I downloaded from Luminescent Pharmaceuticals doesn't make sense. I think I've been staring at the printouts too long."

"Are they one of the companies experimenting with the use of nanotechnology in medical treatments?"

"Yes. They've had some breakthroughs too, or so some of their research would suggest. But the reports I've been looking at today don't back it up. I'm not sure exactly what they do say, to be honest."

"If anyone can figure it out, it's you."

"Right. I'd rather slice vegetables."

"All done, but if you're intent on manual labor, you can start on the dishes."

She looked over to the nearly empty sink. "You're a clean-as-you-go kind of cook, aren't you?"

He shrugged. He liked order. Nothing wrong with that.

She grinned, as if she knew a joke she wasn't telling, but headed over to start on the dishes.

He put the red snapper covered in Cajun spices into the melted butter in the cast-iron frying pan. The fish started to sizzle immediately, the scent of chili powder and crushed red pepper seeds filling the kitchen.

"Smells delicious," she said as she washed the pan he'd used for the sauce. "You're a really good cook, aren't you?"

"It's a hobby."

"A pretty serious hobby, by the look of things."

"It relaxes me." Cooking blackened red snapper with mango-lime sauce was a far cry from MRE rations and helped him to distance his home time from that in the field.

"I like to cook too, but my roommate says I'm too keen on experimentation for my own good."

"How can you help it?"

"That's what I tell Rebekah."

"A fully stocked kitchen's an irresistible temptation to someone with an intimate working knowledge of chemistry. Or so Roman says."

"Roman experiments in the kitchen too?" Danusia sounded shocked by the prospect. "Rebekah is more into physics than chemistry, but she is more than happy to just follow a recipe, you know? I like to try different things. And Roman does that?"

Max nodded, all serious. "They don't all turn out either."

She laughed and this time the sound was pure joy. His cock throbbed in response, and he would have given it a good thump if she wasn't looking right at him.

He settled on turning back to the stove and finishing dinner, tossing the now cooked carrots in a chicken-butter sauce and plating everything while it was still hot.

She was drying her hands when he finished. "Where do you want to eat?"

He didn't really care and said so.

She blushed and looked off to the side. "Um, there's a new show about a superhero family I've been wanting to watch. The dad is one of my favorite actors."

"So, we'll watch it."

"Really? You don't mind, after all the work you put into dinner?"

"Nope, don't mind a bit."

It was so worth the grin that lit her entire pixyish face. And the show wasn't bad. Even better, though, was her reaction to it.

"You've really got a thing for superheroes, don't you?"

She blushed. "With my family, can you blame me?"

"I'd say they'd all consider you more the superhero than them."

"Superbrain maybe, but Elle got the whole package. She's beautiful, smart and she can kick ass too, just like Electra. Then there's Matej, he's not a secret agent like the others, but he's doing such important work, he might as well be Dr. Bruce Banner without the whole Hulk side-effects thing. Mykola has got the super spy thing going on too and then there's Roman."

"A scientist for the Army."

"*Tchya*." The look she gave him told Max that Danusia didn't buy the long held cover story for a minute.

"Let me guess. You think being a military scientist has some super-hero quality to it too?"

"Maybe, maybe not, but you and I both know Roman doesn't work for the Army – at least not as a scientist – nope, he's no more a scientist than I am a cover model."

"Why not a scientist? He's got the degree and the brains.'

"And he carries himself like a soldier, a real soldier, not a lab rat. Roman's too tanned to spend his days in the lab too. And he's got this scary aura, almost as scary as yours."

"You think I'm scarier than Roman?" That would be a first.

"Yes, but maybe that's because I see him through the eyes of his baby sister. I know he'd never willingly or knowingly hurt me." The way she said it made Max wonder if Roman had unknowingly hurt his little sister.

"Who do you think he works for?" The Chief was going to shit kittens when he found out his baby sister wasn't taken in by his cover.

Not one little, tiny bit.

"He told my parents he was speaking at a symposium on Polymer Sciences in Europe. Funny thing, he's not listed as a speaker."

"Maybe they didn't get his name up in time."

"Maybe he's on assignment somewhere else. My guess is out of country, or he would have told them he was going to be somewhere in the States. And he's not in Europe because he would never give his real destination."

Hell, she should be working for the Atrati. "Maybe you've got an overactive imagination."

Hurt flared in her eyes. "Maybe, I'm not as dumb as my family seems to think. I realized Elle was some kind of government agent before her first husband died. I didn't tell anyone else. Little sisters find secrets, they don't share them. I knew when Mykola was working undercover on that drug case. I even knew where he was living, but I'm not about to tell him that. When he couldn't save everybody, I knew he'd be broken and when he showed up at Elle's company, it was obvious there was more going on than anyone wanted to admit."

"What the hell?"

"I use my brain for more than studying."

"I think maybe *you're* the scary one."

She shook her head. "I'm just a little sister that wants to know more about her siblings than they're willing to tell her."

There was a pain in Danusia's voice he understood all too well. He'd heard it often enough in his mother's tone when his daddy had refused to talk about his weeks on the road, saying when he was home he didn't want to think about his time in the truck.

"They all love you." He knew that much from things Roman had said.

"They keep secrets. They share with each other, but think I'm too young to know, or something."

"They're just protecting you."

"They think I'm a security risk."

"You *are* telling me stuff I doubt they want others to know." Not that he considered her a risk, but she needed to be more circumspect, especially when it came to Roman.

Who was in Africa right now on a black-ops mission commissioned by the Army. But Danusia was right, neither Roman nor Max worked for the military anymore. They were agents for the Atrati, a paramilitary organization that did a lot of work for the government but was not under the government's official aegis.

"You're one of them, if not a spook, something super-secret." He opened his mouth, but she put up her hand. "Don't. Don't lie to me. Just don't say anything if all you're going to do is deny it."

He had an insane urge to tell her the truth, which was absolutely not going to happen. "You sure this isn't your superhero obsession playing tricks with your brain?" he asked instead.

She stood up, grabbing her plate and his. "Never mind. I shouldn't have said anything."

"But you did."

"Right. So, I guess I *am* a security risk."

Well, shit.

Chapter Three

Danusia adjusted the hand towel on the rack after wiping down her brother's marble countertops.

She'd insisted on cleaning the kitchen on her own, telling Max that it was only fair since he'd cooked. He'd looked like he was about to argue and she'd given him the look, the one she used on her big brothers and sister when she was absolutely adamant about getting her way.

Max took the hint and left.

Thank goodness for small favors. She couldn't believe she'd set herself up for disappointment like that. He'd been right about one thing; she'd let her imagination run away with her.

Oh, not about her sibs, but about the connection she'd thought she'd made with Max. He might find her sexy; he didn't have a reason to lie about it anyway. But they weren't friends and even if they had sex, they weren't about to become lovers.

Men like him did not have full-on relationships with women like her. The fact was she knew *most* people didn't want to. No matter how hard she tried to fit in, her intelligence made most people give her a wide berth. It was hard to make friends, even in the academic community. She was lucky her roommate had stuck with her through college. Even though Rebekah was four years older than Danusia, she'd never let that get in the way of being the younger woman's friend.

Rebekah was the only person in Danusia's life that didn't push her away, or treat her like she was different, or a freak. In fact, she treated Danusia more like a little sister than her own siblings. The main reason for not going to Rebekah when Danusia realized she didn't want to stay in the apartment alone had been her fear of finally wearing out her welcome with the other woman.

So, she'd come to what she'd believed to be Roman's empty apartment and ended up sharing with Max. The one man who she found more interesting than even her doctoral thesis.

Max was no more interested in being real with Danusia than her brothers and sister. So, what? She was used to being lied to and kept at a distance, wasn't she?

If they weren't smothering her with protectiveness, her family kept her as far away as possible. Even her parents and baba had insisted she attend a university too far away from them for her to live at home.

For her own benefit of course, the physics and chemistry departments were second to none. Thank God, she'd been placed in a room with Rebekah her first semester. Homesick and terrified by the campus living, Danusia had glommed onto a kind and extremely patient Rebekah, who helped the younger girl navigate her strange new world.

Rebekah had steered Danusia toward the lab when she was feeling out of place and taught her that no matter her age, sex, or circumstance, this was somewhere she would always belong.

So, Max wasn't going to be her boyfriend? That wasn't some big surprise, was it? And it didn't mean Danusia had to abandon all the plans she'd been making since showing up in Roman's apartment and discovering it wasn't as empty as she'd expected it to be.

She'd never had good sex, much less any in the amazing category. She just knew Max would be amazing. Even if she wasn't all that great at it. She could learn and a man like him, he could teach her.

She was tired of fantasies and loneliness. She didn't know how long she had in the apartment with Max, but she was going to take advantage of whatever time she did have.

With that in mind, she went looking for her brother's liquor supply. Not that he'd ever offered her a drink, though she'd been of legal age for more than three years now. Everyone in the family except her mom and *baba* treated Danusia like she was still a teenager. Mom and Baba? Wanted her married.

A harsh laugh sounded. Right.

She was better off married to her studies and, one day, to her own research.

She found Roman's alcohol supply in a cabinet in the living room. She supposed it was considered a mini-bar, but all she knew was that he had a truly impressive array of alcohol from all over the world.

Even some good, old fashioned, Ukrainian potato vodka, distilled and bottled by an official distillery even. She was sure there was a bottle of her papa's efforts in there somewhere too, but that was too special to drink on a whim. Or without permission. She pulled the vodka with the black label out of the cabinet and poured a finger each in two high ball glasses.

"Indulging in a nightcap, professor?" Max asked from behind her.

She hadn't heard him come in, but this just meant she didn't have to go looking for him. Turning, with a glass in each hand, she extended one toward him. "Join me."

"I don't know if that's such a good idea." He eyed the drink like a snake set to strike.

Interesting. What did he have to be wary about?

"Sure it is. How can you turn down vodka distilled in Ukraine?"

"Do you swear in Ukrainian like your brother?" he asked instead of answering.

"Sometimes." Worried, she asked. "Do you not drink? Should I have not offered this to you?"

"I can hold my liquor just fine, but every soldier knows better than to drink when they need to keep their head."

"Why do you need to keep your head?" Was he planning on going out?

"I've got five good reasons."

"Care to share them."

"Not really."

She looked at her drink, then back to him, trying to understand his reticence, but respecting it. It might be time to go to Plan B, getting herself tipsy enough she wouldn't care if he was slightly lubricated or not.

Then without warning, Max took the glass and slammed it back like a shot. He held his breath for a second and then let it out slowly. "Those Ukrainian moonshiners know their stuff."

She giggled. Which she never did, and she hadn't even had a drink yet, but she followed his example, swallowing against the burn of the strong distilled alcohol. "Papa says his grandfather made some of the best potato vodka in the world. Good for your liver."

Max gave that ultra sexy laugh again. "Right. Does your father distill his own?"

"I'll never tell."

"You can tell me, I'll keep your secrets." He gave her a serious look, like he was making a promise.

But she wasn't going to read anything into the words. She was done wearing those fantasy inspired rose-colored glasses.

She took his glass and turned back to the cabinet. "Like another?"

"I think one is enough. For both of us."

"You do what you like, but I'm having another. If you don't mind being out drunk by five-feet-six-inches of academia, that's on you."

She poured again, this time two fingers of the clear liquid into her glass and then slammed it back.

Max made a sound that was suspiciously close to a growl and then he grabbed the bottle and poured his own double shot.

He grinned wildly at her. "Here's to Ukrainian brainiacs and Marine grunts."

She didn't call him on the fact that he admitted to being a Marine and her brother was supposedly Army and yet they worked together. She simply nodded and gave him her own crazy smile, the alcohol already hitting her.

He shook his head after. "If I didn't know better, I'd think you were trying to get me drunk to have your way with me."

Smart man. "Is it working?"

"Doesn't matter."

"You don't think?"

"No matter how much I want you, or how drunk you get me, I've got enough control to stop myself screwing my friend's baby sister."

She didn't lie and say Roman wouldn't care. They both knew he would. He wanted her settled down with another brainiac, off in a lab somewhere where she wouldn't worry her family, hence the blind dates from hell.

He didn't want her to get more embroiled in his life, through his *associates*, or any other way. "Don't worry...I won't share your secrets," she said, repeating Max's words.

He shook his head. "Not going to happen."

"That's what I said. You don't have to worry about me telling tales." She wasn't a blabbermouth.

"We're not having sex." Well, that was blunt.

But she could be blunt too. "You want me."

"*Yes.*" That single word held a wealth of meaning.

He really wanted her, like seriously, really. Of course, the growing, and quite impressive, bulge in his jeans said so even more than his affirmative.

"I'm right here." She pulled her t-shirt over her head and dropped it on the floor. Blunt was good. Action was better.

He made a strangled sound in his throat and stepped back. "Ain't going to happen." But his eyes ate her up.

And that was so hot, she couldn't help posing a little. She might have felt stupid but for the alcohol and the way he watched her, like he was a sailor on leave and she was the first woman he'd seen after getting off the ship. No, even hotter...so hot, her skin burned.

Her jeans came off almost as easily as her top. She stepped out of them. "Really?"

She thought maybe it was going to happen. Max's body for sure wanted it, no matter what his mouth said. She stretched and did a little turn. "All yours for the night."

"*Shit. Piss. Damn.* You shouldn't have done that." He spun away and practically sprinted for the guest bedroom.

"Where are you going?" she demanded, even the warmth from the alcohol not equal to the chill of his blatant rejection.

"Bed, where you should go too...in the other room, not mine." He was babbling and it would be cute except for what he was saying. "Goodnight, Danusia," he called over his shoulder as he disappeared down the hall.

Danusia stared down at her nearly naked body. Okay, she wasn't a nearly six foot tall supermodel like her sister, Elle, but she wasn't horrific either. And they hadn't done anything yet, so he couldn't know she wasn't a perfect sex kitten between the sheets.

Oh, she'd be happy to try, but no amount of reading made up for practical experience and hers had been pretty dismal.

Her alcohol muddled mind couldn't decide what she'd done that had sent Max running. He'd said he wanted her. His body had shown it. Oh, how it had shown it.

But he'd also said he had five reasons. *Five reasons for not having sex with her*.

She needed to find out what those were.

Because she wasn't about to give up on the first man that could hold her attention when there was new data to decipher.

Chapter Four

M ax woke to the smell of coffee, and frying ham.

So, the little professor was up and around already.

His stomach growled, reminding him it had been a long time since dinner and he'd slept in later than normal. He'd been awake half the night fighting the urge to go find Danusia and finish what she'd started with her impromptu striptease.

He couldn't get the image of her sexy, pale curves out of his mind and it'd haunted him right into his dreams too.

She might be average in height, but her legs looked long enough to wrap around his hips just right.

The matching sheer blue bra and panties she'd been wearing hadn't left anything to the imagination either. Who would have thought the serious student would wear such sexy lingerie?

He knew her nipples were a deep raspberry red when excited and that while her breasts would be a generous handful, her nipples weren't overly large. He would have so much fun teasing them to swollen hardness though.

Knowing her pubic curls were the exact same chocolate brown shade as the hair on her head only made him want to play down there and see how much darker they looked when wet with her excitement.

His morning hard-on liked the image so much it went from semi-hard to locked, loaded and ready. Shit.

Not what he needed right now.

And she wasn't just sexy, she was sweet and hella smart.

And she'd made coffee. And ham. Which usually meant some kind of eggs as well. His stomach growled again at the thought. Of course there was no saying she'd made enough for him, not after the way he'd rejected her the night before. Running away like the scared little boy Maxwell Baker had never been.

Piss and damn.

She was sitting at the table, drinking a mug of that delicious smelling coffee when he made his way into the kitchen a few minutes later. She looked up and smiled, her expression nothing like what he expected from a woman he'd turned down the night before.

She nodded at a covered plate on the other side of the table. "Your breakfast. It's a good thing you got up when you did. Eggs are just nasty cold."

"You made Eggs Benedict? *For me?*" Where was hers?

"Yep. I prefer fruit and yogurt for breakfast."

He looked pointedly at the empty spot but for her coffee in front of her at the table.

She shrugged. "I ate earlier. I never sleep very late when I drink the night before."

"Really?" He, as a rule, slept later and if he wasn't careful, woke with a headache – even if he hadn't drunk enough to get a hangover.

"Yeah, just another way my brain doesn't work like other people's."

He sat down, pulling the cover off his breakfast. "Looks perfect."

"I followed the recipe."

He caught himself on a chuckle. "That's good, I guess."

She nodded.

He pulled his napkin form under the silverware to put in his lap and noticed a piece of paper under. It was blank except for the numbers one through five.

He looked up at Danusia. She had that look in her eyes again, the one that made him wary. "What's this?"

"You said you had five reasons. I want to know what they are."

"Does it really matter?"

"It does to me."

"Telling you what they are isn't going to change the fact that they exist."

"Refusing to tell me what they are isn't going to change the fact I want you and you want me either."

Well, hell. "Roman didn't tell me you were so stubborn."

"It sounds like he told you plenty, even if he didn't tell you that, which he knows by the way. In case you were wondering." She sipped her coffee. "But, you know, it sounds like you and Roman have talked an awful lot about me."

"I guess." He went for casual, but he knew he'd been caught.

He could see it in her eyes.

She confirmed it with her next words. "I wouldn't think my brother would talk about me much, not without prompting anyway."

"He's proud of you."

"Still..." She gave him a look that dared him to deny asking about her.

He shrugged. "I was curious."

"Because you wanted me."

"You're blunt."

"It's the scientist in me. You're changing the subject."

"Yes." To both. He did want her, and he really wanted to change the subject.

His control had never been so close to the edge. Scared the hell out of him and excited him beyond reason too. It was almost a better adrenaline rush than going on assignment.

Something in her grey gaze said she knew exactly what he'd meant by the yes. She nodded toward the paper with the numbers on it. "So, tell me why you can't have me."

"I'm not writing it down."

"Afraid my brother will find it in the trash after you're gone?"

It was a serious consideration. "Look, if you can't live without knowing, I'll tell you."

"Okay, so talk, but don't let your breakfast get cold."

He started eating and thought about how to approach telling her his reasons. Should he start with the biggest one and try to circumvent the need for the conversation?

The stubborn tilt to her jaw said that wouldn't work.

He decided to start with the reason he figured she'd consider the most valid. She'd already shown she didn't consider the fact she was Roman's baby sister any kind of roadblock. "I'm not in the market for a relationship."

"So?"

What the hell did she mean, *so*? "You're a forever kind of woman."

"Tell that to the other men I've had sex with." She shook her head, her expression nonplused. "I don't think they got the memo."

"You've had sex?" Of course she'd had sex. She was twenty-four, but other than the striptease the night before, she came off as Pure Grade A innocent.

"My family might have sent me away from home when I was thirteen, but they didn't send me to a nunnery."

"You had sex back then?" he asked, feeling queasy.

She grimaced. "No, of course not. I was still a kid, but I've been an adult for six years."

"So, you've had sex." He was still having trouble wrapping his mind around it.

"Yes. Not mind-blowing sex, or even good sex actually, but I have copulated with members of the opposite sex."

"How many?" Oh, shit. "Forget I asked that."

"Why? You wouldn't want me to ask you the same thing?" she guessed.

He winced. "Something like that."

"You're not a man-whore. If you were, you would have taken me up on my offer last night. Regardless of your reasons."

"You have a lot of faith in a man you barely know."

"You think you're the only one who has asked Roman a few subtle questions?"

He wasn't touching that one. "So, the stupid assholes you've had sex with before aside, you still deserve more than a night rolling in the sheets."

"You won't have sex with me because I deserve a relationship?" she asked, sounding really confused and more than a little irritated.

And if that wasn't too damn adorable, he didn't know what was. Which was not the way he was supposed to be thinking.

"That's one of the reasons, yes."

"Since I'm not expecting anything other than that mind-blowing sex I've only ever read about, that particular excuse is voided." She spoke with a firm certainty that showed she knew how to argue for what she needed.

More than that, she expected him to blow her mind?

Who was he kidding? *Blow her mind?* If he got his hands on her, he wasn't going to stop until she was past coherent and right into passing-out-from-pleasure mode.

"You can't just void a reason because you don't like it." He just wished he was as sure as he sounded.

"I can void an excuse that is directly linked to me and *my* feelings. You don't get to make choices for me in that regard. No one does."

He could argue that he got to make choices about his own feelings, but that would be admitting he was experiencing emotions he didn't usually. He'd rather drop the F-bomb during Sunday dinner at his mother's when she had the pastor over.

"We don't even live in the same state," he reminded her.

"It's only a six hour drive, but I don't even see how that excuse has any relevance since we both agree you aren't looking for a relation-ship."

"You should be looking for a relationship."

"Who are you to tell me what I should be looking for?" There was that temper again, flaring in her voice and grey eyes snapping like molten metal. "If I want a break in the monotony of my own company, whatever the cost, don't tell me not to go for it. Because *what I deserve* is a few lousy hours of not being alone."

She should have sounded desperate. Another woman saying it would have, but damned if he didn't find himself agreeing with her instead of pitying her. The fact he was panting to touch her colored his views, he was sure.

Still, he shook his head. "I know you don't think it matters, but Roman is your older brother and he's not only my boss, but he's my friend."

"He's your boss?"

Shit. He never let stuff slip. "Yes."

"Don't look so discombobulated. I told you, I'm good at finding out what I want to."

"Is that what this is about? You're trying to use me to find out more about your brother's life?"

"I wouldn't do that." She jumped up from the table and started wiping down the already clean countertops. "I don't use people."

He knew that. He did. It just wasn't in her nature. She was a sacrifice-to-not-upset-others kind of person.

He got up and went to her, laying one hand on her shoulder. "I believe you."

It wasn't an apology, but he wasn't great at those. Would it be enough?

She turned to face him, her grey eyes swirling with things he couldn't decipher and some that he could. Desire. Pain. Loneliness.

"Your family has no clue, do they?" he asked her before he could stop himself.

She didn't ask what about, she just shook her head.

"They think they did the best for you, sending you off to university at thirteen."

"I was mature for my age, it came from having a really facile brain and siblings that were so much older than me. I told them I didn't need my mom to come with me. It wouldn't have been fair to take her away from my dad. *Baba* would have come, but she didn't move over from the old country until I'd been at university for two years already."

And her parents had believed Danusia when she told them she didn't need them. She'd let them off the hook and they'd swum on happily in their local pond while she tried to find a place for herself in unfamiliar waters.

Unable to help himself touching her, he brushed her hair behind her ear. "You deserve so much more than I can give you."

"I'll take what I can get." Again, the words could have been desperate, but she said them with a calm certainty that blew him away.

He let his hands drop to her waist, his long fingers almost touching
behind her back. "You're so tiny."

"Please tell me that's not one of the five excuses."

"*Reasons*. And no, it's not." Though maybe it should be.

"Good."

"I joined the Marines right out of high school."

She tilted her head back so their gazes were locked. "If that's one of
your five, you're going to have to explain why."

"I didn't go to college."

"Right. So, no fancy degrees for you, huh?"

"Not a one."

"At the risk of sounding like a CD with a skip in it, does that really
matter if you're not looking for a long term relationship?"

"I guess not." It felt like it did with her though.

"But it bothers you."

"Some."

"Not everyone gets their education at a university."

"True."

"You've got life experience I can't begin to match, does that make
you think less of me?"

"No."

"Good."

"It's not the same."

"Oh, I think it is. You read a lot too, don't you?"

"Roman tell you that?"

"I guessed, but he confirmed it. I already know you've taught
yourself to cook like a chef. Degree, or no degree, you're a renaissance
man, Max. And for the record? I've known more academics than most

people. A university degree does not decree instant compatibility, nor does the lack of one mean two people cannot find and maintain common ground. You may not have my brain, but you're a long way from stupid." She smiled up at him. "Unless you really refuse to take me up on my offer, then I'm going to revise my opinion of your IQ."

"Brat."

"Matej calls me that sometimes, but it sounds different coming from you."

"I sure as hell hope so." The temptation to kiss her was so strong, he had to step back.

Only his hands refused to let go, so the distance between them was limited and not real effective.

"Five," she said in a breathy voice that revealed he wasn't the only one effected by their nearness. "You said there were five reasons and you've only given me four so far."

"You're six years younger than me."

She gave him a considering look. "You know, for a man not in the market for a relationship, an awful lot of your excuses are based on your perception of long term compatibility."

He didn't have an answer for that, or at least one that would make sense – to either of them.

"But six years? Really?" she went on, when he didn't say anything to her observation. "Sixteen *might* worry me, twenty-six would give me some doubt, but six? Please. When we were teenagers, those six years would have mattered, but we're both adults now and they just don't."

"I'm thirty and I should have enough self-control to keep my hands off you."

"But you don't?" she asked hopefully.

He found himself grinning as the inevitability of what was going to happen between them washed over him. "I don't."

And if she wasn't convinced by his reasons, he wasn't going to hang onto them like a sulky child. She was right, this was just sex and if she wasn't pushing for more, who *was* he to insist she should?

"Seriously?" she asked.

"Oh, yeah."

"Now?"

He shook his head. "You have work to do today."

"It's the weekend, I can take some time off," she said suggestively.

"I'm teaching a class this morning. I need to be there in forty minutes, but I'll be done by three," he said quickly when her face fell.

He would call in and cancel class, but he wanted her to have some time without him around to think about what he'd said and change her mind if she was going to.

"Hm...not feeling like working. Maybe I'll get a massage."

"I guarantee you'll get plenty of touching when I get back."

"That's what I'm hoping, but to maximize the experience, I should work on getting relaxed." He couldn't tell if she was joking, or not.

Scientists didn't think like normal people. Roman might be more soldier than scientist now, but the man still proved the rule.

Then he realized why she was so tense. "The break-in threw you, didn't it?"

"It scared me, yes."

He should have realized, but she'd done that thing with him that she clearly did with her family. Pretended to be okay when she was frightened and facing the unknown. He wasn't going to fall for it again. "Why didn't you go stay with family?"

"Everyone but Roman is in a fairly new relationship. They don't need me horning in on their privacy."

"And your parents."

"Would you go stay with *your parents*?"

"Point taken." He loved his mom, but he preferred to get a hotel room when he went to visit her.

"So, three o'clock?"

"I'll be here by three-thirty."

"Yum."

Laughing, he shook his head. "You're sweet."

"You think?" She fluttered her lashes outrageously and he laughed again.

Giving into the urge that had been riding him since walking into the kitchen, he leaned down and gave her a brief, but thorough, kiss.

He ran his tongue along her lips to savor her flavor before pulling back. "A little taste of what's to come."

She just nodded, her expression dazed.

Sex between them was definitely going to be mind-blowing.

He was whistling when he got in his car.

Chapter Five

Danusia rolled the pencil between her teeth, the faint taste of wood comforting in its familiarity.

Her roommate, Rebekah, teased Danusia for using the old-fashioned, yellow *No. 2* pencils that had to be sharpened every morning before she started work. Danusia firmly maintained a mechanical pencil was not the same. She grabbed the *No. 2* and put a check beside another anomaly in the research.

These results simply did not make sense in the face of the company's claims of a breakthrough in nanotechnology for medical treatment.

She put the pencil back in her mouth and flipped to the next paper in the stack. This one listed results exactly as she'd expected them to be. Her brows drawn together, she put the two printouts side by side.

A big warm hand landed on her shoulder and she gasped, spitting the pencil out. It clattered as it bumpily rolled across her brother's glass tabletop.

Her heart galloping, she jumped up and spun, knowing on one level that it had to be Max and another not so sure.

It was him and he was smiling. "You know, after this morning, I expected a little different reaction to my return."

She looked around frantically for her cell phone, the only "watch" she ever wore, but it must be buried under the papers she'd been reading. "Um, is it that late already?"

"Later."

Then she noticed his black hair was damp and he was wearing PT shorts that exposed the full of his dark, muscular legs. No shoes, and no shirt. Oh, man.

Her legs wobbled.

The man had a to-die-for chest. "You took a shower."

Without her, darn it!

"I did." He tugged her ponytail. "No massage?"

"Oh, I was going to call and then got to thinking about something I wanted to check in my research..." she trailed off, embarrassed. "Um, how long have you been here?"

"A while. When you didn't respond to my initial greeting, I found you studying in here." He looked around the dining room she'd taken over for her work area.

"Roman's desk isn't big enough to spread out on." She bit her lip. Like Max cared where she studied.

"You get really lost when you're working, don't you?"

No use denying it. "Yes."

"That could be dangerous."

"I don't study away from my apartment at night." When all of her older siblings kept harping on it, she'd finally promised them she would do her library work earlier in the day.

"It's cute."

"Seriously, you're not irritated?"

"Nope." And he didn't look mad either. Not even a little annoyed.

"Oh." Cool.

"You looked pretty intent when I first got here, and not very happy."

"It's these results." She indicated the printouts on the table. "They're supposed to show Luminescent Pharmaceutical's breakthroughs, but they're pretty much the opposite."

"You think Luminescent is making false claims for their research?"

"They could be. Maybe this data is older, but they're really sloppy about some stuff. It's hard to tell."

"What do you mean?"

"They keep meticulous records of results, but there are no dates anywhere on three of these reports, or names for the projects. It's odd."

"It sounds suspicious, if you ask me."

"Yeah, that's what worries me. Luminescent is a major supplier for pharmaceuticals for third world countries and the Middle East. If they're supplying products that don't work, but make things worse, that's..." words failed her.

"Dangerous."

"Right." Not to mention, unethical. Despicable. Just plain rotten.

"I mean, dangerous for you."

"What? Why for me?"

"You've got to wonder if you were supposed to be given this set of data."

He had a point. "The woman helping me get the downloads was a little ditzy." Then it was like Danusia's brain finally switched on and she shook her head. "What are we doing talking about my research?"

"Just discussing our days, right?"

He wanted to do the how-was-your-day thing? It was her own fault, so she bucked up and asked how his was.

He laughed. "If you could see your face, professor. My class was a wash. I nearly sent two of the participants to the infirmary."

"That doesn't happen very often?"

"Try never."

"Why today?" she prompted, wanting him to say it.

"Wasn't paying enough attention to pull my punches properly."

"Oh." She liked hearing that. A lot.

"Yes, *oh*. Want to take a guess what I was thinking about?"

"Your best friend's Bar Mitzvah?" she couldn't help teasing. She was feeling giddy.

"Not Jewish and neither is he."

"The government cover-up of alien visitations?"

"Not a conspiracy nut."

Her research said it wasn't so *nutty*, but that was a discussion for a different day.

She was grinning as he reeled her into his body. "How best to utilize your retirement fund?"

"Brat." Then he kissed her and all desire to tease fled, along with coherent thought.

His mouth fit perfectly over hers. His lips gave just the right pressure to send tingles of awareness radiating outward, until she could feel this one perfect kiss in her toes. She responded, letting her tongue dart out to taste. He groaned and suddenly their tongues were sliding against each other and his arms were around her, pressing their bodies together.

His skin was so warm and soft under her hands, his muscles so hard.

She caressed along his sides, around his back and back over his chest, loving the feel of his curly chest hair under her fingers. Her hands could not stay still though. They sought out one treasure after another. Hard male nipples, well defined pecs, biceps that bulged under her fingertips, inviting her to grip them tight and hard.

She mapped his every bulge and valley of muscle with the investigative fervency of an obsessed topographer.

This man could so easily become her obsession, probably was already, if she was honest with herself. And she did try to be.

She couldn't believe she could touch and feel to her heart's content. Was there such a thing? She didn't think she would ever grow tired of caressing this man, her desire to touch never completely sated.

His hair was cut Marine short, the high and tight even more compact than on other men because of Max's tight nap. It felt amazingly sexy against her palms, and she writhed against him, her hands on his head, pulling him closer, moaning into the kiss.

His arm made a shelf under her buttocks and then he lifted. They were moving, his hold on her strong, his mouth masterful.

Both their eyes were open, but while his were watching where he carried her, hers were fixed on him. He was just so incredibly gorgeous and even more so with that look of desire in his sherry brown eyes.

She landed on the guest room bed with him on top of her. And wasn't that just perfect?

He thrust his hips against her, his hard-on pressing, teasing, making her whimper. "You're wearing too many clothes, professor."

She'd heard that word tens of thousands of times in her academic career, sometimes directed at others, sometimes at herself. Never before had it sounded like a synonym for sweetheart.

"So're you." Naked would be good. Oh, yes. Really, really good.

He gave that delicious laugh even as he started unbuttoning her blouse. He pulled it open and then gave a low whistle. "Nice."

She wiggled out of the top. "Nice would be naked."

He nodded, moving so he could get her jeans too. She didn't like wearing shoes or socks, if she could get away with it, so he didn't have any hindrance to pulling the jeans right off. Other than the fact that they were the tightest pair she owned, but that didn't seem to bother his efforts even a little.

She'd never gotten this particular pair of pants off as fast.

When they were gone, he stopped and just shook his head. *"Damn."*

It sounded more like *damn fine* than a curse so she let him look his fill without worrying what he was thinking.

"I like the panties." She was wearing a fire-engine red thong. "But you're missing your bra today, professor."

"I thought it might help my cause." That and her tight jeans. She could admit she'd brought them with, in the extremely off-chance she somehow saw Max while she'd been in Boston.

"You really are a brat."

"Determined."

"Calculating."

"A scientist knows to take the right tools into the lab."

"You consider your breasts tools?"

"In attracting you, I sure hope so."

"You're so damn refreshing."

"That's better than irritating."

"Not the same at all."

"I'm glad."

"I'm horny."

She burst out laughing. "Then, I guess you better do something about it."

"You take off those tiny little panties and I just might."

"Might?" she asked with a teasing look as she hooked her thumbs in the waistband and started pushing down.

"Will."

"Better."

She tossed her thong away and then waited for him to do the same to his shorts. Only he hadn't moved a muscle and his gaze was fixed on her nudity. "You're exactly like I dreamed."

"You had dreams about me?"

"I did."

"I had dreams about you too. That means something, don't you think?"

"It means we should have made it like bunnies at your sister's wedding."

She found herself laughing again as he pushed his shorts off. Her laughter ended on a choked gasp as she got her first glimpse of his hard penis.

Okay, so her previous two encounters had been with much smaller men overall, but Max wasn't just big. He was huge.

"You got a license for that thing?" she asked on another choked laugh.

He prowled toward her. "It'd have to be a Class OIC #3 for large weapons."

"You've got that right." Was he even going to fit?

She was going to try. Really, really hard. And like she'd told him, she was very determined.

He climbed up onto the bed, slinking over her until his body completely dwarfed hers, his hardened flesh a hot brand against the apex of her thighs and up her stomach.

Definitely big. Really, really.

"You okay, professor?"

"Oh, yes." More than. Really.

"You sure?"

"Why do you ask?"

"You keep saying *really* over and over again."

"Oh, um…it's just a word." And she'd been thinking out loud again. *Aargh.*

"And you are just adorable."

Again, huge improvement over how her other sex partners had seen her – as irritating.

She leaned up to kiss him for that. He responded immediately, his mouth molding to hers in that way that felt so, so perfect. This time, he didn't stop at her lips though.

He kissed down her neck, paying close attention to where it joined her shoulder, sending chills of pleasure along her nerve endings. Then he moved down to her collar bone, using his tongue tip to trace along each clavicle bone before lapping between her breasts. She'd never realized she was sensitive there, but he showed her she was and so much more.

He avoided her breasts and the small bit of flesh pulsing with a hungry need for touch between the folds of her labia.

Only when she was breathlessly begging for, "More, more, more, please, more, just more, please, Max!" did he move to take one nipple between his lips.

He nipped it gently and then laved it with his tongue. She gasped out a sound more animal than woman; it was certainly one she'd never heard herself make before.

He started suckling, while bringing his hand up to cup her other breast and roll that nipple between his fingers.

It was an overload of pleasure, and she felt tremors she only recognized as a different kind of orgasm as they crested and she found herself shouting his name and several Ukrainian naughty words.

Oh, wow. *Wow. Wow. Wow!*

Suddenly long, thick, masculine fingers were delving into the wet flesh between her legs. He pressed one into her vagina and crooked it, curving upward. He rubbed and hit a spot that she'd read about but never discovered on her own.

She screamed again, this time a wordless sound of pure need.

He reared back. "You ready for me?"

"More than."

He nodded, leaning over her to grab stuff from the bedside table. When he kneeled up again, he had a condom in his hand. "Want to put it on me?"

"Yes."

She sat up and put her hand out for the condom packet. She fumbled, but managed to get it open and the condom out intact. Then she stopped. "I want to touch you."

"Later," he growled out as he tugged her hand toward him.

She nodded. Later. Yes. Lots of touching later, but now? He was going to be inside her.

First though? She needed to taste, just a little. She touched his weeping slit, and then brought her finger to her mouth. Salty. Sweet. All man.

He groaned.

She moaned.

"Put it on me," he demanded.

She nodded again, this time frantically. Yes, yes, yes. Hands shaking, she rolled the condom down his big erection, squeezing a little as she went. Oh, man. Her fingertips didn't quite touch as they circled him at the base.

She whimpered. "Want you."

"Lay back, sweetheart. I'm all yours."

Falling back, she spread her legs, bending her knees to make all the room he needed between her thighs.

"Damn, you are one sexy braniac." His dark gaze burned through her.

"Uh-huh." Whatever. She just wanted him inside. Now.

He laughed, even as he moved into position, his head right at her entrance. "You're thinking out loud again."

"I do that sometimes." She arched up, trying to get him to come inside.

"I've noticed." He pushed forward, just a little. "It's cute."

"Max! Come on."

That dark chuckle sounded again and then he was pushing inside, stretching tender intimate tissue to capacity.

"Feels so good," she gasped out.

"Oh, yeah."

He made little rocking motions with his hips, pushing deeper with each small thrust.

She felt like she was going to fly apart, and he wasn't even all the way inside.

"Me too," he ground out, making her realize she'd done it again.

Good thing he didn't find her habits irritating.

"Not irritating. Sexy. Oh, shit." His big body shuddered as he bottomed out inside her.

Their eyes locked, neither of them moved. The moment felt too profound. It was supposed to be just sex, but there was something going on here, something she didn't even know could happen. But she felt like at this moment, they were one being.

The look of intense concentration on his face said he felt the same, or at least something close to it.

She opened her mouth to say something, she didn't know what, but he shook his head. And started to move.

Strong hands gripped her buttocks, tilting her pelvis just so and that tingle inducing spot inside her vagina got stimulated on the long, slow glide out and then in again.

He didn't speak. She couldn't. He moved in and out, one slow thrust after another.

She'd thought she'd wanted hot, hard and fast, but this was so good. *So perfect.* The pleasure built, and built, and built, and she never wanted it to end.

"Gonna do this for hours," he said.

"Next time." Because even with the slow thrusts, she knew she wasn't going to last long.

And he was already so swollen and hard inside her, he had to be close too.

"Next time," he agreed as the thrust of his hips increased in tempo.

Unable to do much, the way he had her tilted, she strained against him. "Want it. Want it. Want it," she chanted over and over again, knowing that blissful release was just over the next rise.

Then he locked her knees over his arms and pressed her legs further apart while thrusting deeper than he'd done yet.

She felt her climax explode through her, taking her in wave after wave of drowning bliss. She screamed. She cried. And she came. And she came again.

Her body wasn't even hers anymore; it belonged to pleasure.

A hoarse, masculine shout sounded above her and his body went rigid. She was so sensitive, she could feel the pulse of his erection as he came too.

She wondered what it would be like without the condom, without any barrier between them.

"Dangerous, professor, damn dangerous."

Oh, man. She *had* to stop thinking out loud, or she was going to tell him she was falling for him...*had fallen for him* and in a way that was anything but casual.

Chapter Six

They were cuddling together in his bed after a delicious bout of shower sex when her cell phone rang.

She flung her arm out toward the sound, but the rest of her body didn't follow. "You broke me."

"You complaining?" He stroked his hand along her flank, leaving shivers of sensation in his wake despite her total satiation.

"No."

"Didn't think so."

"I should get that."

"Later." He didn't make a move to incite more sex, though, but pulled her closer into the curve of his body. "We need a nap."

And that? Was really dangerous.

#

Danusia listened to the message her apartment manager had left on her phone for the second time, trying to convince herself it said what she'd thought she'd heard. But it was just so wild.

Max sauntered in from the kitchen. He'd insisted on making dinner again, saying cornbread crust pizza was a no-brainer and she could work on her thesis while he threw it together.

He'd made it pretty clear he didn't want her help, so she'd come into the dining room. The research wasn't making any more sense than it had earlier, and she'd remembered the phone call earlier. Listening to her messages seemed like a legitimate reason to procrastinate.

Only the message didn't make any more sense than the printouts littering the table.

"What's the matter?" he asked.

"What? Oh..." She closed her phone and stared at the opposite wall, wondering if she should head back to her place tonight, or wait for morning.

Ever since they'd woken from their nap, Max had been putting distance between them. She got that. The sex between them had been too intense and he'd made it clear he wasn't looking for a relationship.

It still hurt.

"Danusia?" he asked, sounding wary.

She turned to look at him. "I need to get back to my apartment."

He didn't look disappointed, or happy, or well *anything*. Max had his game face on, and she had no hope of reading it.

"The super get the door fixed?" he asked.

She filtered the message her manager had left through her brain for an answer to that question. "Yes, with a super deadbolt and an interior security flip bar."

"Sounds like they're taking your safety seriously."

They should. Her apartment had been broken into a second time, but left totally trashed on this occasion. The thieves, vandals...wha tever...had disabled the security alarm this time. Elle was going to be pissed.

All Danusia said was, "Yes."

"When are you going?"

"I was thinking about heading back tonight." The police wanted to talk to her and needed her to go through her place and see what had been taken.

His head jerked, his game face gone in the wake of dark emotion. "Tonight? What's the rush?"

"There's no reason to put it off."

He frowned and then got that sexy look she found so irresistible. "I can think of a few."

"Really?"

"If you leave now, you'll be driving into the wee hours. That's not safe. Don't even pretend to think that's a good idea for a woman alone."

That was so not where she'd expected him to go. And he was right, but she was feeling reckless. She just shrugged.

His eyes narrowed, but all he said was, "You don't want to miss my pizza."

"It's that good, huh?"

"It is."

She sighed, knowing his first argument was a valid one, especially in the light of what had happened at her apartment. "I guess."

"Do you really want to give up one more night of this?" he asked, indicating himself.

Finally, he went where she'd thought he was going to begin with, but maybe it was good he hadn't started out with the sex, which was so much more than just sex. At least for her.

And she would have said for him too.

But she was the first to admit her ability to read men was nothing like her skills in the lab.

"Conceited," she accused.

"You saying I don't have reason?"

"No."

"So?"

She wasn't sure her heart could handle more of the kind of sex they had together. And what came after.

Her leaving. And him letting her go.

He stepped toward her, his expression predatory. "You don't look convinced."

"I might need a little persuasion." Her heart might not survive this intact, but it was already cracking around the edges.

At least one more night in his arms, was one more night before she had to let the pain in. Before the loneliness took over.

And it wasn't as if she didn't know how to deal with being alone.

"I think I can do that." He pulled her gently up from the chair, taking her phone and laying it on the table before wrapping her in his arms.

He lowered his head. "The pizza's got fifteen more minutes. I can do a lot of convincing in that amount of time."

"You'd better get to it then."

"Oh, I plan to."

Then he did. The kiss was incendiary and her worries about her heart melted in its heat. She reached up and locked her hands behind his neck and threw herself into it. Maybe it was that she'd never kissed a man she found so attractive, or maybe it was simply kissing this man, but every time their lips locked, she lost herself.

He lifted her against him, pressing that impressive hard-on into the apex of her thighs. It wasn't enough.

She wrapped her legs around his hips and rubbed against him, unable to stifle the sounds of frustration when that just made the ache worse.

He broke his mouth away from hers. "Shhh, sexy, I'll take care of you."

Then he sat down in the chair she'd been using, standing her up between his thighs. He unsnapped her jeans and lowered the zipper. "Let's get rid of these."

"Yes." She shoved the denim down her legs and kicked it away.

He grasped her hips, his hands so big that his thumbs easily reached her clitoris through the nylon of her panties. He brushed over the aching nub first with one thumb and then the other, teasing and satisfying with the same touch.

"Touch me, Max."

"I am touching you, professor."

"You know..." her voice failed as he rubbed a little circle over that spot.

"I do, yes."

Suddenly, her panties were gone and then she was sitting astride his lap, facing away from him. He tilted her head back so he could kiss her while his other hand moved between her thighs.

He brushed his fingers up the sensitive skin of her inner thigh before delving into her most intimate flesh. He slid one long finger inside her while his heel pressed against her swollen clitoris.

She moaned into the kiss, her body arching toward that touch, her brain losing touch with reality in a maelstrom of pleasure. She didn't know how long he touched her like that, but the faint sound of a buzzer sounded from the kitchen just as her body and mind exploded like nanobots in a microwave. Sparkly lights behind her eyelids while she cried out against his lips.

\#

Dinner was delicious, but what happened after was mind destroying. He yelled her name when he came and held her throughout the night. She woke before dawn, knowing she needed to get going before she did something really stupid, like ask him to come with her. Or if she could come back.

She was in the shower when she heard her phone ring. It stopped by the time she'd turned off the water and reached for a towel.

She was still drying herself off when Max walked into the bathroom looking pissed off and too darn sexy for this early in the morning.

"You want to explain to me why I just got off the phone with a police detective who wants to know when you'll be back in town?"

She wrapped the towel around herself and tried sidling toward the door, but Max wasn't moving. She stopped in front of him. "It's about the break-in."

"Like hell. The police don't follow up like this on an attempted break-in when the perp didn't even make it inside the apartment."

"Not the first time."

"What the hell happened?"

"Do you think I could go to Roman's room and get some clothes?" Her backpack was still in the master bedroom.

Max leaned against the door jamb. "Talk."

"You're bossier than all my older siblings combined."

"You think?"

"They never grill me naked."

"You're wearing a towel and I'm your lover. That comes with certain privileges."

"You're my current sex partner; that's not the same thing."

"I'm not done with you yet."

"Right. I'd say we're done. I'm going back to my apartment, and I don't see you making a six hour drive for a booty call."

"You plan to go back to an apartment that's been broken into twice now, *alone?*" His volume rose with each word until he was as loud as her dad watching the Super Bowl.

She made a show of shaking her finger in her ear. "Loud, much?"

"Tell me what is going on." He bit each word out with a jaw like granite.

So, she told him.

He didn't look any happier once she'd explained it than when he'd been in the dark. In fact, there was a muscle ticking in his jaw now and his breathing was even only by force of will. She could tell.

"Man, you really are worse than Roman."

"Like hell you are going back there alone," he said instead of responding to her accusation.

"I have to go back. The police need to know if anything has been stolen and I don't want them calling Rebekah and upsetting her."

"Your roommate can stay just where she is."

Since Danusia agreed, she didn't say anything.

"I'll go with you."

"What? No. No way. I'm an adult, I can take care of this."

"It's either take me, or I call your parents and your sister and two brothers that are in the country right now."

"You don't have their numbers."

He held up the phone. "I do now."

"You're being ridiculous."

"Which will it be?"

"You can't just take off from work like that. You've probably got some super-soldier mission to go out on."

He flipped the phone open. "Make your choice."

"Fine. Gosh. If I'd known all it would take to get you to go with me was to get my apartment broken into, I would have done it sooner," she said sarcastically, hoping he couldn't hear the strain of truth in her voice.

He heard something, because he shook his head and turned with a heartfelt, "Shit," as he went back into the guest bedroom.

"You don't have to go with me," she called after him. "I could call my sister."

Because really? Two break-ins? Not normal. Danusia and Rebekah had chosen their apartment partly because of the building security and safe neighborhood.

"Don't start with me, Danusia Lyudmyla Chernichenko," he yelled from the other room.

"You know my middle name?" she asked on a squeak as she hurried into the bedroom, her hand clutched in her towel.

He spun around to face her, a pair of black cargo pants in his hand. "I know a lot about you, your middle name's the least of it."

"It's not my fault. My grandmother's best friend back in the Old Country was named Lyudmyla."

He just gave her a look.

"It's embarrassing. So old fashioned."

"It's cute, like the rest of you. Now, go get dressed."

She would have found it more of a compliment if he wasn't barking at her like a drill sergeant.

She saluted smartly and scurried from the room. He caught up with her halfway down the hall. He spun her around and slammed his mouth down on hers.

He didn't kiss her long, but when he finished, she was gasping and dazed. "Brat."

She nodded before she realized what she was agreeing to and then shrugged. "If you're good at something..." She left the rest unsaid.

"I'm good at killing people."

This time she knew exactly why she was nodding.

"I was MARSOC."

"Marines special forces."

"Yes."

"Sniper or assassin?"

"Does it matter? I was and am a human weapon."

"Maybe it's time for a career change."

"Maybe it's not." There was a question in his words, but she wasn't sure he was even aware it was there.

She just leaned up and kissed him softly. "I'll get dressed."

Chapter Seven

They made the six hour drive in five and still managed to talk nearly nonstop the whole time. Danusia told Max about what it was like to grow up out of sync with her peers and in a family of such loving, overprotective, and yet distant siblings.

Max told her about growing up on the fringe of his middle-class schoolmates with a long-haul trucker for a father. His mother hadn't handled the separations well. When Max told her he'd never heard the woman laugh until several months after his father's death, when she'd started seeing a widowed school teacher, Danusia had felt tears burn her eyes.

"You think no woman could handle a relationship filled with absences."

"No woman should have to."

"Military wives do it all the time. Other long-haul truckers have happy marriages."

"The divorce rate in the military, especially any special forces branch, is significantly higher than national averages. Same for long-haul trucking."

"It's still possible."

He'd changed the subject, but she was beginning to see how a man who based most of his excuses for not getting involved on stuff that would only matter in a relationship could say he was only interested in casual sex.

#

Max looked for anyone or anything out of the ordinary as he walked slightly to the side and behind Danusia into her apartment building. There were security cameras in the parking lot and the entrance.

If the perps hadn't been caught on them, that meant one of two things. Lucky or professional. He knew which one he was leaning toward.

Danusia lived on the third floor and her apartment was at the end of the hall. Again, the fact she was furthest from the elevator and stairwell increased the perps' chances of being seen.

"No news on who broke in?" he asked, pretty sure he knew the answer already.

"None. Two men wearing dark hoodies were seen on the security cameras, but their faces were never visible."

"And no one noticed suspicious persons loitering outside your apartment?"

"The police said they don't have any leads."

He didn't say anything else as they met up with the manager outside Danusia's door.

The woman wearing a red power suit let them in. "I don't know what's going on. This is highly irregular," she said, giving Danusia an accusing glare.

"What is irregular was your superintendent's careless attitude about putting a new door in. This second break-in could well have been prevented." Which he actually doubted, but hell if he was going to stand by while the snooty bitch tried to make Danusia feel responsible.

His little professor didn't seem to be paying attention to either of them. Her focus was on the chaos on the other side of the now open door.

Danusia walked slowly inside, her head swiveling to take in what was clearly a very thorough job done on turning her apartment. Shit.

This was no robbery. Someone had been looking for something. And they hadn't found it, or the entire place wouldn't be so methodically trashed.

#

Which is what he said to the detective when he and Danusia stopped by the police station later.

"That was our take as well, Mr. Baker."

Max frowned. "And you didn't warn Danusia? Why the hell not? She could have walked right into something."

The detective gave Danusia what was no doubt supposed to be an intimidating frown. "In our experience, when someone is looking for something with that much determination, the person in possession of that something is already aware of the fact."

"We as in who, detective?" Danusia asked. "Your police department? How many cases of this sort have you investigated? Enough to make an acceptable statistical average?"

"I'll ask the questions here, Miss Chenko."

"It's Chernichenko and you may call me Danusia if that's easier."

"What were the perps looking for?" the detective asked.

"I don't know for sure."

"Look, Danusia, we can't help you if you won't be frank with us. If you're in something over your head, we'll do what we can to help, but you need to tell us what it is."

"Local police are allowed to lie." She turned to Max. "Only federal investigators are required to tell the truth, though that doesn't extend to the CIA apparently."

Max almost laughed, but he held it in. "Do you think Rebekah is involved in something dangerous?" he forced himself to ask.

"No, but I think I may be."

The detective looked triumphant.

Max should have been surprised, but he wasn't. "The pharmaceutical research?"

"Yes. I realized in the car on the way here what those results could indicate. I mean, if you weren't looking for people getting better."

"What's that?"

"Nanotechnology as a weapon rather than medical treatment."

He cursed. The detective looked confused, and he didn't look like he understood a whole lot better after Danusia's explanation. To give the guy credit – which Max wasn't overly inclined to do considering his negligent attitude toward Danusia's safety – parts of her explanation went right over Max's head as well.

But he had no trouble figuring out that his little professor was in a world of trouble. Or would be if he weren't around to keep her safe. He didn't just know how to kill people, he knew how to stop others from doing it.

He planned to put his knowledge and experience to full use in protecting the sweet and too damn sexy scientist in the making.

And it was a damn good thing, because once the detective did get the gist of what Danusia was trying to tell him, he immediately dismissed her theories as farfetched and fanciful. "This isn't an episode of *Law & Order*, Miss Chernko."

Max couldn't decide if the man was getting her name wrong on purpose or really was that dense.

"I'm fully aware that this is real life. It's my apartment that's been ransacked, detective."

"And you want me to believe someone did it trying to get back a bunch of computer data you got researching for your paper." The man couldn't have come off as more dismissive if he'd called her *little lady* and rolled his eyes.

"Do you have a better theory?" Danusia asked.

But Max didn't need to.

"Well, now. It's a lot more likely that you've been turning your knowledge of chemistry to more lucrative endeavors." The police detective's words were annoying as hell but expected.

Danusia, though, looked shocked and horrified by the implications. "You think I've been making drugs?" she demanded, proving her brains worked outside the classroom too. "Are you aware that one of my brothers is a former DEA agent?"

"Former?"

"Oh, my gosh, I can't believe what you are implying." She turned to Max. "Is he really saying what I think he's saying?"

"Looks that way to me."

"Now, listen here, Miss Chenkiro."

The detective's misuse of her name yet again was the last straw because she gave him a contemptuous look and got to her feet, marching away from his desk toward the exit without another word.

The detective wasn't so quiet. "Wait a minute, there. You can't go storming off. I'll have you arrested on obstruction of justice."

Danusia ignored the petty threat for the empty hot air it was.

The man jumped up to follow her, but Max got between them. "If you'd found drugs in her apartment, she'd already be under arrest. You've fucked up this investigation and any chance of a promotion you might have gotten out of it."

With that, he left, catching up with Danusia before she was out of the building.

"That man is an idiot."

"He lacks imagination."

"Oh, I'd say he's got plenty of that."

"No, for him, it's same old, same old. He can't wrap his mind around a crime that isn't centered on drugs or domestic violence."

"He thought I was making drugs." She sounded so furious and so hurt.

Max put his arm around her shoulder, even as he maintained easy access to his concealed weapon. "It wasn't personal, sweetheart."

"It felt personal."

"I know."

"Do you?"

"Sure. I've been pulled over for nothing more than DWB."

"What's that?"

"Driving while black."

She didn't laugh like he expected. "That's terrible."

"Hey, it happens to teenagers too. No matter how much they deny it, law enforcement profiles."

She stopped three cars down from where they'd parked and looked up at him, eyes swimming with hurt. "Do I *look* like a drug dealer? Maker? Whatever?"

"Now, *you're* profiling."

"Yeah, I guess. I don't like it, and I don't know what to do." Her lower lip jutted and he felt like a heel because all he wanted to do was nibble on it. "I'll have to call my family," she said in the next breath, her tone about as happy as new recruits told they had an extra hour of PT before mealtime.

"No, you don't."

"I don't?"

"I'll call in some friends."

"Like Roman did for Elle's wedding."

"Something like that." But this situation was going to take official government involvement.

"Why would you do that?"

"You're too smart for stupid questions, sweetheart."

"I was right."

"About what?"

"*Professor* does sound just like *sweetheart* the way you say it."

#

Danusia lay on the bed and flipped through the complimentary newspaper in their hotel suite an hour later while Max made phone calls in the other room. He'd insisted it wasn't safe to stay in her apartment and she hadn't argued. She'd left their accommodations up to him and wasn't surprised to find herself in a suite at the end of the hall on the seventh floor of a hotel with both a doorman and twenty-four-hour reception desk.

She expected other men like Roman and Max to show up any minute and set up some kind of security plan for her. If it were her family doing this, she knew she'd feel stifled and like somehow, she was inconveniencing them. Even if they would deny it. But with Max? She felt protected. Almost cherished.

It was crazy, considering how he insisted they didn't have a future, but the man was way too worried about her feelings and safety for a casual lay.

She idly flipped to the Metro section to see what was going on around the city when a small article on the lower left corner caught her eye. The picture was one of those awful ones used for drivers licenses and employee identifications. It was of the woman who had given Danusia the data for her thesis at Luminescent Pharmaceuticals.

And she was dead.

She'd been involved in a single car accident at freeway speeds late at night. No witnesses. The article said the roads had been slick with an unexpected summer rain and it was unclear whether she'd fallen asleep at the wheel or simply lost control of her vehicle.

What were the chances?

Danusia grabbed the Metro section and rushed into the sitting room. "Max."

"Hold on," he said into the phone and looked at her. "What's up, professor?"

She handed him the paper. "That woman, down at the bottom of the page? She's the one that gave me the data at Luminescent."

Max's eyes narrowed and he read the brief article lead before swearing. "Our timeline just amped up," he barked into the phone. "They're not just trying to get the data back. They're eliminating loose ends."

Danusia couldn't hear what the person on the other end of the call said and wouldn't have understood if she had. Her brain was going into meltdown. She was so not superspy material like her sister.

The thought of someone wanting her dead scared the pee out of her. Well, not literally. But it was close.

Oh, man. She was babbling, even in her head.

Strong arms wrapped around her and Max's body heat broke the chill of terror trying to take hold. "It's going to be okay, sweetheart. I'm not going to let anything happen to you."

She clutched at him. "I'm scared. I shouldn't be scared."

"Who says? This is scary shit."

She almost laughed. "You're not scared."

"You're wrong."

She reared back so she could see the truth in his face and sure enough there was a shadow of worry in his eyes, which was probably as close to really frightened this man got. "I don't understand."

"I'm damn good at my job. Both of them. Killing and protecting."

"So?"

"So, I've never been personally invested in keeping my client alive."

"I'm not your client. I'm your lover." He'd said it first. He could deal with it.

His head dropped to rest against hers. "I know."

"I think that scares you more than the thought of the bad guys getting past you." She'd meant it as a tease.

But his fierce frown said he didn't get the joke. "Not even close."

"Okay."

"But I've never had one," he said.

"A lover?"

"Yeah."

"You're no virgin."

"Neither are you."

But she'd never had a lover before either. She got it. Sex partners yes, lover no. The difference between them? She *wanted* a relationship. She didn't want to be alone, though she'd proven to herself and anyone else who cared to take note that she did just fine that way.

She'd been raised in a close-knit family with parents who loved each other deeply. She wanted that for herself. She wanted someone to call her own. Not someone. She wanted this man. He wasn't ready to hear that though. She wasn't sure he ever would be.

"It's going to be okay," it was her turn to comfort.

This time he did laugh, though the sound wasn't his usual sexy joy. "A couple of friends are coming in by helicopter. They should be here in an hour."

"I guessed. Should I pretend I don't realize they're some kind of black-ops group?"

"Paramilitary black-ops is the correct term."

Something inside her cracked at this little tidbit of honesty. "Is it?"

"Yes."

"And?"

"They won't tell you their real names. You don't have to pretend you don't realize what they are or why they're here. Our nicknames are used for a reason other than to piss some of us off." He sighed. "Though you'll probably learn some of them eventually if you hang around me long enough."

"Am I going to be hanging around?" she asked.

"Long distance relationships have a pretty bad success rate."

"Is this a relationship?"

"I don't know." He looked so pained, so frustrated, she didn't push.

"We'll focus on the problem at hand right now," she offered.

His game face came over his features like a robot mask. "Right. That's exactly what we should be doing."

She went to step out of his arms, but he didn't let her go, tugging her over to the couch instead. He sat down and pulled her right into his lap.

"*This* is focusing on our problem?"

"Part of my job is making you feel safe right now."

"I do feel safe."

"You saying sitting in my lap doesn't make you feel safer?"

"No, I'm not saying that." It didn't make sense, because really it shouldn't make any difference, but she didn't want to move.

"Good."

"What now?"

"The big boss is making some phone calls. They'll need the data
and your interpretation of it, but then the spooks will move in on
Luminescent Pharmaceuticals."

She snuggled more firmly into his lap. "What's your role in all this?"

"Keeping you safe."

"Don't you want to be in on the takedown?" she asked, as she
rubbed her head against his shoulder.

"I want to be your hands-on bodyguard." It sounded like a promise
of something else entirely.

She decided to go for the joke, rather than press for him to ac-
knowledge what he was really saying...if he was saying what it felt like.
"Sounds dirty."

"Sexy maybe."

"Sexy definitely."

"Good."

"Speaking of sex."

"We've got forty-three minutes until the others arrive."

"Let's not waste it."

And they didn't. Though he did insist on taking a few minutes
to set up some complicated contraptions on the windows and door
before carrying her off to bed and once again blowing her mind with
pleasure.

Chapter Eight

His friends turned out to be a lot like she'd expected. Which meant they reminded her of Roman and Max. Though one of them was a woman. They set up a rotation of guards, but Max stayed with her all the time.

Someone else might have gotten sick of spending so much time in a hotel suite, but she was used to working on her thesis for days at a time. Besides, she had the distraction of Max.

Totally delicious and wonderful, he used sex to help her work off any tension she built up being in the same two rooms. She didn't need to go running when he loved her into a puddle of exhausted pleasure. Sex, the perfect cardio.

They kept talking, too, about their more recent pasts and their hopes for the future.

"So, you want to be doing this when you're ninety?" she asked him at one point.

He shook his head. "Nah. Can't do what I do when you lose your game."

"So, what does your future look like?"

"There's a pretty high mortality rate in my profession."

"You plan to be dead?"

"Hell, no."

"Then?"

Well, that answered the question of whether a black man could blush. He could. And it was adorable.

"What? With a reaction like that you can't not tell me."

"You know I like to cook."

"You want to be a chef?" She wasn't seeing why that would embarrass him.

"I want to own my own place."

"You want to open a restaurant."

"Nothing big. Not fancy-assed. Something that only serves breakfast and lunch."

"Like a diner."

"More like a deli, but not."

"One of those little food carts?" Maybe he thought former Marines should do something more dangerous, but she thought he'd be really amazing at this.

He loved to feed her...the suite had a mini kitchen, and he did most of the cooking.

"That, or a little coffee shop style place. Though I'm not looking at serving a bunch of fancy-assed coffees either. There are enough places that do that already. Not in Boston, but maybe in California. Mama and her teacher moved there a few years ago and they do enjoy the sunshine."

"Where in California?"

When he named a town only about thirty minutes from the one her parents lived in, Danusia felt the inevitability of destiny shiver across her soul.

#

Max hung up the phone as Danusia stood up and stretched from where she'd been working hunched over the suite's fairly ample desk for the past six hours. He'd never seen anyone get so lost in deskwork for so long, well except maybe Spazz, but he was too antsy not to get up every hour or so and work off a little of his extreme extra energy.

Her pretty breasts pressed against her top, her nipples hardening as she moved in response to the now flowing blood in her body probably. She turned to him and caught him looking.

He grinned. "Nice view."

"I'm glad you're enjoying the perks of babysitting me."

"Professor, I can guarantee you I don't see you as a child."

She smiled and sauntered forward, putting a sexy sway in her hips she only did around him. He liked it. And he liked that she did it for him. "I need to go to the library."

"Too dangerous."

"How long are we going to be here?" she asked, though he could tell she wanted to argue about the library.

"The spooks are setting up a sting at your apartment. Making it look like you're moving back in. They want the hit team."

"That tells me what they're doing. Not how long it will take."

"There's no way of telling, but we don't have to stay here, professor."

"I'm not taking this trouble back to Roman's place. What if they find me there?"

"My condo is ready, and the movers delivered my furniture to-day." He'd been thinking about taking her back to Boston since the threat level escalated with the Luminescent employee's death, but he'd known Danusia wouldn't go for returning to her brother's apartment.

She looked at him, waiting for more.

"Come stay with me."

"I..." She looked over his shoulder, though he knew there wasn't a damn thing of interest to see.

"You said you're defending in October. Does that mean you aren't signed up to help with classes in the fall?" he asked her.

"Yes."

"So, you're just working on your thesis?"

"Yes."

"Does it have to be done here?"

"The university library is here."

"And you still need it?"

"Not exactly."

"Why the trip today then?"

"I want to verify some facts and a couple of resources."

"Sounds like busy work."

"I'm ready to get out of this suite."

She'd lasted longer than a lot of people would have. "I get that."

"So?"

"So, come home with me."

"For how long?"

Shit. He knew this question was coming and damned if he hadn't decided what his answer was going to be. "For as long as I can get you to stay."

"You mean like in sickness, health, and corrupt pharmaceutical companies trying to get to me?" she asked, as her gaze came back to him.

"Yeah, like that."

"I..." She was looking at him again, but her eyes were filmed with tears. "I thought you didn't want a relationship."

"I want you."

"Any way you can get me?"

"Pretty much, but damned if I'll settle for casual."

"You sound like a man who knows what he wants." She sounded like a woman who wanted what he did.

"I am."

"And love?" she asked.

"It comes with the package."

"You're not going to say it?"

Damn it. He opened his mouth but closed it again. He hadn't said those words to anyone in his adult life. Last time he'd said it to his mom he'd been about ten years old. They weren't a kissy-huggy-tell-you-I-love-you-all-the-damn-time family.

Danusia smiled, but shook her head. "We'll go to your place for now. We'll work out the details later."

That was better than he expected after all the times he claimed he didn't want a relationship. She didn't ask for explanations. She didn't demand those three words he found so hard to say.

She was perfect for him.

\#

They flew back to Boston in the helicopter. Danusia left her car for the female agent baiting the trap for the hit team to use. They settled into a routine. She worked on her thesis during the day, and he went into the Atrati headquarters every day to his job when stateside.

The hit team took the bait three days after the female agent moved into Danusia's apartment pretending to be her. Nothing was said by either of them about her returning to her apartment. One drawer in his dresser held her clothes as well as some hangers in the closet.

His spare bedroom had become an office with an oversized desk and overflowing bookshelves.

The spooks wanted Danusia's help building their case against Luminescent. She gave it, though he knew it put her behind in her thesis.

When Roman's team went off the grid in Africa, Max didn't hide it from Danusia, trusting her to keep silent about it. Just like she'd managed to not give even a hint to her own involvement in an illegally developed weapons case at the federal level, or the fact she'd been the target for a hit team, despite several phone calls with family.

Her mother wanted a visit. He was thinking on that. On what to do about visiting his own family and getting to know Danusia's...be sides Roman anyway.

Then a team with his name on it got assigned a job in South America and Max had to make a choice.

\#

Danusia was just sending some more support documentation off to the US Attorney General's office for the case against Luminescent Pharmaceuticals when she heard Max arrive. He wasn't due home for three more hours.

A sinking feeling in the pit of her stomach, she went looking for him. She'd been waiting for this day since coming back to Boston with Max. She was sure she knew what was coming. They found each other in the hall outside the room he'd given her to make into an office.

The serious expression in his eyes made her stomach clench. "What's going on, Max?"

"I got an assignment. South America. Fly out oh-four-hundred."

She nodded, her throat tight, her mouth suddenly so dry, she didn't know how she was going to force words out, but she had to. This was where their relationship moved forward or broke forever. "I'll get the rest of my stuff moved in here while you're gone."

Something moved in his dark brown eyes, something like hope and joy. "You didn't ask how long I'd be gone."

"It doesn't matter. I'll be waiting here for you when you come home."

"This is home for you?"

"Wherever you're going to be when you're not working, that's home for me."

"Oh, God." And it was a prayer not a curse the way he said it. He pulled her tight against him, in a way that had become familiar. "I love you, Danusia."

"I love you too, Max, so much." Hot tears ran down her cheeks.

He'd finally said the words and hers had been the right ones. He didn't want to get rid of her. He wanted her to stay. He really *wanted* her.

"I refused the assignment."

"What? You? What?" She couldn't breathe for the happiness blooming inside her. She was scared to trust it, but his dark gaze made promises.

"I'm not leaving you. You're my family. My dad, maybe long-haul trucking was all he knew. Maybe it's all he wanted. But damn, him and my mom? They weren't happy. Maybe they wouldn't have been even if he was home the other twenty-two days of the month, but I want a family with you...a life that includes time together."

"I thought you weren't ready to retire from soldiering."

"I thought I wasn't either, then I met you."

He wasn't going to leave her alone. She meant so much to him that he was going to change his life for her. Danusia felt the happiness burst in her chest and she started laughing, even as the tears still tracked wetly down her cheeks.

He picked her up and carried her into the bedroom.

"You really like carrying me."

"Just call me Power Man."

She giggled as he dropped her on the bed. "I'd rather call you Max. You're the man I love."

He leaned down to kiss her, his lips right against hers as he said, "I love you. Always."

After they made love (which was so much more fun than packing him up to leave the country and put his life on the line again), she was snuggled into his side, drowsing when he asked, "Once you finish this PhD thing, how do you feel about moving to California, closer to our families?"

"You're really serious about us, aren't you?"

"I refused any more field assignments, I'd say so, yes."

She grinned against his dark, warm skin. Every time he said it, she loved hearing it – as much as hearing his *I love you's*.

"Matej and Elle's company has already made me an offer of employment. I wasn't sure about it, though it's exactly the kind of place I feel I could make the best income." Maybe she could build closer, more normal relationships with her siblings now that they were all adults and the age gap and the brain gap just wasn't that important anymore.

He squeezed her tight, his hand settling on her hip. "We're going to do it, aren't we, sweetheart?"

"What?"

"Work on that happily ever after so many people talk about."

"Yes, yes, I think we are."

THE END

If you enjoyed Tight Spaces, please consider leaving a review, or rating. Thank you!

With more than 10 million copies of my books in print worldwide (Isn't that wild?), I'm an award winning and USA Today bestselling author with over 90 published books. My stories have been translated for sale all over the world and after a long career in traditional publishing, I've gone indie. I am loving the freedom to write the stories both me and my readers enjoy the most. My new steamy mafia romance series, Syndicate Rules features the morally gray alpha heroes and spice I love to write. I write contemporary, historical and paranormal romance. Some of my books have action adventure and intrigue. All of them are spicy and deeply emotional. I'm a voracious reader and love to talk about both my books and those I've read (or should read...good recs are always welcome) on social media. Welcome to my world where love conquers all, but not easily!

For info on my books and series extras, visit my website:
www.lucymonroe.com

Follow me on Social Media:
Facebook: LucyMonroe.Romance
Instagram: lucymonroeromance
Pinterest: lucymonroebooks
goodreads: Lucy Monroe
YouTube: @LucyMonroeBooks

ALSO BY LUCY MONROE

Syndicate Rules

CONVENIENT MAFIA WIFE
URGENT VOWS
DEMANDING MOB BOSS
RUTHLESS ENFORCER
BRUTAL CAPO
FORCED VOWS
ASSASSIN'S OBSESSION

Mercenaries & Spies

READY, WILLING & AND ABLE
SATISFACTION GUARANTEED
DEAL WITH THIS
THE SPY WHO WANTS ME
WATCH OVER ME
CLOSE QUARTERS
HEAT SEEKER

CHANGE THE GAME
WIN THE GAME

Passionate Billionaires & Royalty

THE MAHARAJAH'S BILLIONAIRE HEIR

BLACKMAILED BY THE BILLIONAIRE
HER OFF LIMITS PRINCE
CINDERELLA'S JILTED BILLIONAIRE
HER GREEK BILLIONAIRE
SCORSOLINI BABY SCANDAL
THE REAL DEAL
WILD HEAT (Connected to Hot Alaska Nights - Not a Billionaire)
HOT ALASKA NIGHTS
3 Brides for 3 Bad Boys Trilogy
RAND, COLTON & CARTER

Harlequin Presents

THE GREEK TYCOON'S ULTIMATUM
THE ITALIAN'S SUITABLE WIFE
THE BILLIONAIRE'S PREGNANT MISTRESS
THE SHEIKH'S BARTERED BRIDE
THE GREEK'S INNOCENT VIRGIN
BLACKMAILED INTO MARRIAGE
THE GREEK'S CHRISTMAS BABY
WEDDING VOW OF REVENGE
THE PRINCE'S VIRGIN WIFE
HIS ROYAL LOVE-CHILD
THE SCORSOLINI MARRIAGE BARGAIN
THE PLAYBOY'S SEDUCTION
PREGNANCY OF PASSION
THE SICILIAN'S MARRIAGE ARRANGEMENT
BOUGHT: THE GREEK'S BRIDE
TAKEN: THE SPANIARD'S VIRGIN
HOT DESERT NIGHTS

THE RANCHER'S RULES
FORBIDDEN: THE BILLIONAIRE'S
VIRGIN PRINCESS
HOUSEKEEPER TO THE MILLIONAIRE
HIRED: THE SHEIKH'S SECRETARY MISTRESS
VALENTINO'S LOVE-CHILD
THE LATIN LOVER 2-IN-1 with
THE GREEK TYCOON'S INHERITED BRIDE
THE SHY BRIDE
THE GREEK'S PREGNANT LOVER
FOR DUTY'S SAKE
HEART OF A DESERT WARRIOR
NOT JUST THE GREEK'S WIFE
ONE NIGHT HEIR
PRINCE OF SECRETS
MILLION DOLLAR CHRISTMAS PROPOSAL
SHEIKH'S SCANDAL
AN HEIRESS FOR HIS EMPIRE
A VIRGIN FOR HIS PRIZE
2017 CHRISTMAS CODA: The Greek Tycoons
KOSTA'S CONVENIENT BRIDE
THE SPANIARD'S PLEASURABLE VENGEANCE
AFTER THE BILLIONAIRE'S WEDDING VOWS
QUEEN BY ROYAL APPOINTMENT
HIS MAJESTY'S HIDDEN HEIR
THE COST OF THEIR ROYAL FLING

Anthologies & Novellas

SILVER BELLA

DELICIOUS: Moon Magnetism
by Lori Foster, et. al.
HE'S THE ONE: Seducing Tabby
by Linda Lael Miller, et. al.
THE POWER OF LOVE: No Angel
by Lori Foster, et. al.
BODYGUARDS IN BED:
Who's Been Sleeping in my Brother's Bed?
by Lucy Monroe et. al.

Historical Romance

ANNABELLE'S COURTSHIP
The Langley Family Trilogy
TOUCH ME, TEMPT ME & TAKE ME
MASQUERADE IN EGYPT

Paranormal Romance

Children of the Moon Novels
MOON AWAKENING
MOON CRAVING
MOON BURNING
DRAGON'S MOON
ENTHRALLED anthology: Ecstasy Under the Moon
WARRIOR'S MOON
VIKING'S MOON
DESERT MOON
HIGHLANDER'S MOON

Montana Wolves
COME MOONRISE
MONTANA MOON

End Matter for eBooks

Want to read bonus content and to be kept up to date on her books?
Sign up for Lucy Monroe's newsletter on her website:
https://lucymonroe.com

If you enjoyed this book, please consider leaving a review, or rating.
Thank you!
Read the rest of the books in The Goddard Project series:
https://www.amazon.com/dp/B07J2W12YG
Give Lucy's spicy mafia romance series, Syndicate Rules, a try:
https://www.amazon.com/dp/B0C9YTMLZ5
Steamy billionaire romance by Lucy Monroe:
https://www.amazon.com/dp/B0BLT4668B